3 9077 08093 2356

THIRD-GRADE DETECTIVES

The Secret of the Wooden Witness

DISCARD

BRIDGE

J
STA

04/13/16

Stanley, George E.

Third Grade Detectives: #8:
The secret of the wooden
witness   CHILDREN

D1491249

APR 1 3 2016

356

THIRD-GRADE DETECTIVES

DETECTIVES

The Secret of the Wooden Witness

By **GEORGE E. STANLEY**

Illustrated by **SALVATORE MURDOCCA**

ALADDIN · New York London Toronto Sydney New Delhi

FAIRPORT PUBLIC LIBRARY
1 VILLAGE LANDING
FAIRPORT, NY 14450

If you purchased this book without a cover, you should be aware
that this book is stolen property. It was reported as "unsold
and destroyed" to the publisher, and neither the author nor the
publisher has received any payment for this "stripped book."

This book is a work of fiction. Any references to historical events,
real people, or real locales are used fictitiously. Other names,
characters, places, and incidents are the product of the author's
imagination, and any resemblance to actual events or locales or
persons, living or dead, is entirely coincidental.

First Aladdin Paperbacks edition March 2004

Text copyright © 2004 by George Edward Stanley
Illustrations copyright © 2004 by Salvatore Murdocca

ALADDIN PAPERBACKS
An imprint of Simon & Schuster Children's Publishing Division
1230 Avenue of the Americas, New York, NY 10020

All rights reserved, including the right of
reproduction in whole or in part in any form.

Designed by Lisa Vega
The text of this book was set in 12-point Lino Letter.
Printed in the United States of America
8 10 9 7
0414 OFF
Library of Congress Control Number 2003106432
ISBN 0-689-86487-6

To Kathy Slack and her third-grade class at Ottawa Elementary School in Petoskey, Michigan: Petoskey High School Class of 2012! Keep reading and solving mysteries!

Chapter One

Todd Sloan was in the kitchen.

His grandmother had told him he could fix a peanut butter and jelly sandwich for a snack.

But Todd couldn't decide which kind of jelly he wanted: grape, plum, or red raspberry.

Just then his grandmother shouted, "Todd! Come quick! You need to see this!"

Todd raced into the living room.

His grandmother was sitting in front of the television.

She always stayed with him until his parents got home from work.

Todd saw Dr. Smiley's face on the screen.

Dr. Smiley and Todd's teacher, Mr. Merlin, were friends.

Dr. Smiley was also an important police officer.

Todd's class was known as the Third-Grade Detectives.

Sometimes Dr. Smiley helped them solve local mysteries.

"Dr. Smiley is moving to another town," his grandmother said.

Todd stared at her. "She can't do that!" he said.

He looked back at the television screen.

Now they were showing pictures of a PTA talent show.

Todd didn't want to see little kids dancing. He wanted to hear more about Dr. Smiley.

"I'm sorry, Todd," his grandmother said. "They'll probably have more information about her on the later news."

Todd couldn't wait for that.

He had to find out right away what was happening.

He went back to the kitchen.

He dialed Noelle Trocoderro's number.

Noelle was his best friend in Mr. Merlin's class.

When Noelle answered, Todd said, "Dr. Smiley is leaving! She's moving to another town."

Noelle gasped. "How do you know that?" she asked.

"I saw her on television," Todd said.

"This is bad for the Third-Grade Detectives, Noelle!

"I think we need to have an emergency meeting right now."

"I can't, Todd," Noelle said.

"I have to go with my mother to Greene's Department Store.

"Do you want to come with us?"

Todd didn't really like shopping with Noelle and her mother.

It was so boring.

But he had to talk to Noelle about Dr. Smiley.

They had to figure out what to do.

"I'm sure my grandmother will say yes," Todd said.

"Good!" Noelle said. "We'll be by your house in ten minutes."

Todd told his grandmother that Noelle and her mother had invited him to go to Greene's Department Store with them.

His grandmother said it was okay.

Todd was standing on the front porch when Mrs. Trocoderro pulled into his driveway.

He climbed into the backseat with Noelle.

For several minutes they whispered about Dr. Smiley.

Finally Noelle said, "Mom? Why would Dr. Smiley move to another town?"

"She probably got a better job," Mrs. Trocoderro said.

"How could it be *better*?" Noelle asked.

"She has a laboratory in the basement of her house.

"She has a fan club.

"She has the Third-Grade Detectives to help her solve crimes."

"The new job might pay more money," Mrs. Trocoderro said.

"But what will Mr. Merlin do?" Todd asked. "I always thought he and Dr. Smiley were a couple."

Mrs. Trocoderro shrugged. "Well, maybe Mr. Merlin will be leaving too," she said.

"Oh no!" Noelle said.

"What will happen to the Third-Grade Detectives if *both* Mr. Merlin and Dr. Smiley leave?" Todd asked.

Chapter Two

Mrs. Trocoderro pulled into the parking lot of Greene's Department Store.

"Todd and I want to sit in the car and talk about the future of the Third-Grade Detectives," Noelle said.

"That's not a good idea," Mrs. Trocoderro said. "I'd rather you do your talking where I can see you."

So Todd and Noelle reluctantly got out of the car and followed Mrs. Trocoderro inside the store.

Mrs. Trocoderro went to the credit department. "I have to get a couple of gift certificates," she said. "This shouldn't take too long."

"Okay," Noelle said.

She and Todd sat down on a big sofa to wait.

"Is this the end of the Third-Grade Detectives, Todd?" Noelle asked.

Todd thought for a minute. "I guess it doesn't have to be," he said.

"We could set up our own police laboratory.

"We could ask our parents to give us microscopes for our birthdays."

"Say! That's not a bad idea," Noelle said. "Amber Lee would probably let us use her basement."

Todd shivered. He remembered how full of spiders it was. "I think we should put it somewhere else," he said.

"But what if Mr. Merlin leaves too?" Noelle asked. "Will our new teacher still let us be the Third-Grade Detectives?"

Todd shrugged. "A new teacher probably wouldn't know any secret codes," he said. "It wouldn't be the same."

They sighed at the same time.

Just then an elderly man walked past. He had a bandage on his head.

"Pops Verner!" Todd called.

Pops Verner stopped. "Well, if it isn't my two favorite detectives," he said.

Pops Verner used to be a police officer. Now he was the night watchman for the department store.

Pops Verner liked to hear all about the mysteries they had solved.

"What happened to you?" Noelle asked.

"Somebody hit me over the head and stole my pocket watch," Pops Verner said. He thought for a minute. "It's a mystery. Maybe the Third-Grade Detectives can help me solve it."

"We'll be glad to," Noelle said, "but we'll have to hurry."

Pops Verner blinked. "Why?"

"Mr. Merlin and Dr. Smiley are leaving town," Todd said. "The Third-Grade Detectives may not be around much longer."

"Oh, that's too bad," Pops Verner said.

"It sure is," Noelle said.

"Tell us everything that happened," Todd said.

Pops Verner sat down beside them. "Well, the store was closed, and I had started making my rounds," he began.

"I walk through the entire building once every hour.

"When I got to the storeroom at the back,

the lights were off. They should have been on.

"Just as my hand touched the switch, somebody hit me over the head.

"It knocked me out.

"When I came to, the lights were on, and there was a little wooden statue of an old man lying next to me.

"It looked like something someone had whittled in his spare time.

"I was sure that was what had made the knot on my head.

"I got up and walked through the store.

"I thought whoever did it might still be there, stealing things.

"I didn't find anybody, but there was a lot of stuff missing. Jewelry, clothes, television sets.

"So I called the manager, and she called the police.

"They came and made a list of all the things that had been stolen.

"Right before they left, I discovered my pocket watch was gone.

"It was really old. It belonged to my grandfather.

"I gave the police a description of it, but they don't think I'll ever get it back."

"Why not?" Noelle asked.

"They're sure the crook plans to sell what he stole from the store," Pops Verner replied. "But they said whoever took the pocket watch probably plans to keep it."

"That's terrible," Todd said.

"It sure is," Noelle agreed.

"What happened to the little wooden statue?" Todd asked.

"The police took it," Pops Verner said.

"Do they have any suspects?" Noelle asked.

"I told them I thought it might be one of the three new guys who work in the storeroom," Pops Verner said. "Joe, Phil, or Bobby."

"An *inside* job?" Todd asked.

Pops Verner nodded. "All three of them recently moved to town," he said. "I think one of them may have taken the job so he could steal stuff."

"Are they friends?" Noelle asked.

Pops Verner shook his head. "No," he said. "They hardly talk to one another."

"What makes you think one of them had something to do with this robbery?" Todd asked.

"Well, you see, there are lots of places in the storeroom where a person can hide," Pops Verner said.

"The police found little shavings of wood behind a stack of big boxes.

"I'm sure that's where the crook whittled on the little statue while he waited for the store to close.

"So I think that either Joe, Phil, or Bobby hid there until all the employees—except me—had left.

"All three of them deny they had anything to do with it, but I know one of them is guilty!" Pops Verner tapped the side of his head with a finger. *"Instinct!"*

"Well, we'll solve this mystery for you, Pops!" Todd said. "We'll get your pocket watch back for you."

"I knew I could count on the Third-Grade Detectives," Pops Verner said.

Chapter Three

Pops Verner disappeared through a door just as Noelle's mother finished buying her gift certificates.

"Wasn't that your friend the night watchman?" Mrs. Trocoderro asked.

"Yes," Noelle said.

"What happened to his head?" Mrs. Trocoderro asked.

"Somebody hit him with a little wooden statue and stole his pocket watch," Noelle told her.

"He wants us to help him get it back," Todd said.

"Well, if anybody can do that, it's the Third-Grade Detectives," Mrs. Trocoderro said.

The next morning Todd and Noelle walked to school together.

During the night a bad storm had blown down a lot of trees.

They passed people who were sawing fallen trees into small logs.

"I think it's really neat how trees have all those circles inside them," Noelle said.

"Yeah," Todd agreed. "It's like a puzzle."

Suddenly Noelle stopped. "Todd! I just thought of something," she said. "What if Mr. Merlin has already left?" She gulped. "That would be awful!"

"It sure would," Todd agreed.

"I remember the first day of school," Noelle began.

"Our teacher was supposed to be Mrs. Trumble.

"Instead of her, Mr. Merlin was in the classroom.

"I was so disappointed when I saw him. But he turned out to be the best teacher ever!"

"Come on! Let's hurry!" Todd said. "If Mr. Merlin hasn't already left, then maybe we can talk him out of going!"

They started running down the sidewalk.

Finally they reached the school.

They raced across the playground and up the front steps.

They ran to their classroom.

Amber Lee, Misty, and Leon were sitting at their desks.

They looked sad.

"Dr. Smiley is leaving," Amber Lee sniffed. "I saw it on television."

"So did I," Todd said.

"I can't believe Dr. Smiley would do something like that," Misty said.

"Mr. Merlin is leaving too," Noelle said. "My mother said so."

Amber Lee, Misty, and Leon gasped.

"When?" Amber Lee asked.

"We're not sure," Todd said. He looked around the room. "Have you seen him this morning?"

"Yes," Leon said. "He went to put some boxes in his car."

"Oh no, Todd! We're too late!" Noelle cried. "Now we'll never solve Pops Verner's mystery!"

"Noelle! Look! It's Mr. Merlin!" Todd shouted.

He was pointing to the window. "He's in the teachers' parking lot! We can still catch him!"

"Come on, everybody!" Noelle shouted. "The future of the Third-Grade Detectives depends on this!"

They all raced out of the classroom, down the hall, and out the back door of the school.

JoAnn Dickens was just coming into the building. "What's wrong?" she called.

Noelle told her.

JoAnn dropped her books and started running with them.

The Third-Grade Detectives began yelling as loudly as they could.

"Mr. Merlin! Mr. Merlin! Don't leave! Don't leave!"

When they finally reached Mr. Merlin, he gave them a strange look and asked, "What's wrong?"

"You can't leave today!" Noelle said.

"We need your help to solve another mystery before you move away!" Todd said.

Chapter Four

Mr. Merlin looked puzzled.

A crowd of other students had gathered around him and the Third-Grade Detectives.

"If you leave, we won't be the Third-Grade Detectives anymore," Todd said.

"Who said I was leaving?" Mr. Merlin asked.

"Noelle's mother," Amber Lee replied.

Mr. Merlin turned to Noelle. "Is that true?" he asked.

Noelle nodded. "She said that since Dr. Smiley was moving, you'd probably move too," she replied.

"But you can't leave until we solve Pops Verner's mystery," Todd said.

Just then the first bell rang.

FAIRPORT PUBLIC LIBRARY
1 VILLAGE LANDING
FAIRPORT, NY 14450

356

Mr. Merlin let out a big sigh. "Come on, everyone. We don't want to be tardy," he said. "We'll talk about this inside."

The crowd of students headed for the school building.

Mr. Merlin and the Third-Grade Detectives went to their classroom.

When everyone was seated, Mr. Merlin said, "There's been a big misunderstanding.

"It must have started when some of you saw on television that Dr. Smiley has a new job in another town."

Todd nodded. "I called Noelle and told her," he said.

"Well, I'm sad that she's leaving, because I'll miss her very much," Mr. Merlin continued. "We'll all miss her, in fact. *But I'm staying here.*"

The class cheered.

"Then why did Noelle's mother say you were moving?" Amber Lee demanded.

"Yeah!" Leon said. "That's terrible!"

Everyone started talking at once.

"Class! Class!" Mr. Merlin said. "Settle down!"

Everyone stopped talking.

"I can explain this," Mr. Merlin said. "It's something the police have to face every day.

"Even though I wasn't there, I think I know exactly what happened."

He looked at Todd and Noelle.

"Correct me if I'm wrong," he said.

"Okay," Noelle said.

"There's a game you can play," Mr. Merlin began. "It's called Telephone.

"The first person whispers a story to the second person.

"The second person whispers the story to the third person.

"You go around the room until you reach the last person.

"Then the last person repeats the story out loud.

"Usually the story has changed a lot, because in our minds, we just keep adding or dropping details."

"We weren't whispering anything to anybody," Leon said.

"That may be true, but in your heads the story kept changing," Mr. Merlin told him.

"Todd saw the story about Dr. Smiley on television.

"He told Noelle.

"Todd and Noelle talked to Mrs. Trocoderro about it.

"Mrs. Trocoderro said that I might be moving too.

"The more Todd and Noelle thought about it, the more real it became.

"When they got to school this morning, they heard I was taking some boxes to my car.

"That only added to the story that I was leaving town.

"When this happens to the police, they have to decide between the truth and what people have made up in their heads."

"That's exactly how it happened," Noelle said.

"We're glad you're not moving, Mr. Merlin!" Todd said. "Now we can solve Pops Verner's mystery!"

"How can we solve a mystery without Dr. Smiley?" Amber Lee asked. "We always use the laboratory in her basement."

"Well, sometimes we don't need microscopes

to solve a crime, Amber Lee," Mr. Merlin said. "Let's just see what happens before we get too upset about it."

"Okay," Amber Lee said.

Todd told the class Pops Verner's story.

"We promised him that the Third-Grade Detectives would get his pocket watch back."

Mr. Merlin thought for a minute. "Well, Johnny and I will give you a secret code clue to help," he said.

"Who's Johnny?" Todd asked.

Mr. Merlin grinned. "He's one of my spy friends who makes up secret codes," he said.

Mr. Merlin used to be a spy.

He told the Third-Grade Detectives that solving secret codes helped their brains work better.

Mr. Merlin picked up a piece of chalk.

On the board, he wrote: TIGUI BGZ I FYZPRB LYKFXMN.

Todd copied it down as fast as he could.

He wanted to solve the secret code clue right away—just in case Mr. Merlin changed his mind about moving.

Chapter Five

Just then Mrs. Franklin, the principal's secretary, opened the door.

She motioned for Mr. Merlin.

He walked over to her.

Mrs. Franklin whispered something in Mr. Merlin's ear.

Todd thought Mr. Merlin looked really upset.

"Get out your math worksheets, everyone," Mr. Merlin said. "Do all of the problems."

Todd quickly raised his hand.

Had Mr. Merlin forgotten that he had just given them a secret code clue?

Mr. Merlin always let them work on it for a few minutes before they started their school-work.

But Mr. Merlin didn't pay any attention to Todd's hand.

Mr. Merlin quickly whispered something to Mrs. Franklin and rushed out of the room.

When Mrs. Franklin finally saw Todd's hand, she said, "Yes?"

Todd told her about the secret code clue.

Mrs. Franklin said, "I don't know anything about that. I just know that Mr. Merlin told you to do your math worksheets. So that's what I think you should do."

Todd was puzzled.

He turned to Noelle.

She looked puzzled too.

Something was really wrong here, Todd decided.

Mr. Merlin had told them that he wasn't leaving. But he had just left.

Had Mr. Merlin changed his mind? Had he decided to move after all?

Todd leaned over to Noelle. He whispered those questions to her.

"Oh no!"

Todd looked up.

Misty had heard what he said to Noelle.

"Mr. Merlin changed his mind!" Misty told the class. "He's decided to move after all!"

Everyone in the classroom started talking at once.

"He promised us that he was staying!"

"This is awful!"

"How could Mr. Merlin do such a thing?"

Mrs. Franklin stood up. She opened her mouth. But nothing came out.

Todd was sure that Mrs. Franklin couldn't think of anything to say. So he stood up too.

"It's my fault, Mrs. Franklin," he said.

"We don't really know that Mr. Merlin is leaving.

"My head just made it up, and it all came out of my mouth!"

Mrs. Franklin looked even more confused.

"Mr. Merlin explained to us how it happens," Todd continued.

"That's why the police have to be very careful when they hear stuff from people."

Todd turned to the class. "Mr. Merlin told us

that he wasn't leaving," he said. "So we should believe him."

Mrs. Franklin nodded.

But Mr. Merlin wasn't back when the recess bell rang.

Amber Lee was the one who noticed that his car was gone from the parking lot.

Todd quickly called an emergency meeting of the Third-Grade Detectives.

"Maybe I was wrong about Mr. Merlin. I guess we shouldn't have believed him after all," he told them. "We're on our own now."

The Third-Grade Detectives nodded.

"We can't give up, though, because there are a lot of people who need our help," Todd added.

"Pops Verner is counting on us," Noelle reminded them.

"Has anyone solved the secret code yet?" Todd asked.

No one had.

Now Todd was even more concerned.

If the Third-Grade Detectives had trouble

solving the secret code clue, Mr. Merlin always gave them a hint to help.

But Mr. Merlin wasn't there anymore.

Todd knew that somehow they'd have to figure out a way to solve the secret code clue all by themselves.

Chapter Six

When Todd and Noelle got to school the next morning, there was a strange man standing at the front of the classroom.

Todd thought he looked liked a professional athlete.

He had on a T-shirt and shorts. He had a whistle around his neck. He was wearing tennis shoes.

He didn't look anything like Mr. Merlin.

"Good morning," the man said. "I'm Coach Hawkins."

"I think we're in trouble," Todd whispered to Noelle as they took their seats.

"Why?" Noelle asked.

"I don't think Coach Hawkins will be interested in how police use science to solve crimes,"

Todd said. "He'll probably want to talk about sports all the time."

Todd was right.

They used basketball scores in math.

"If Texas Tech scored 85 points and Minnesota scored 76 points, by how many points would Texas Tech win?" Coach Hawkins asked.

Misty raised her hand. "Nine," she said sadly.

They studied the names of college mascots in spelling: RED RAIDERS, GOLDEN GOPHERS, SOONERS, WILDCATS, and BULLDOGS.

Amber Lee got them all right. But she didn't seem very excited about it.

In reading, Coach Hawkins gave them stories about the lives of famous athletes: TIGER WOODS, VENUS WILLIAMS, MARK McGWIRE, TROY AIKMAN, and MICHAEL JORDAN.

Leon read the stories faster than anyone else.

So Coach Hawkins gave him five gold stars.

But Leon stuck them to his forehead instead of putting them by his name on the reading chart.

Finally the recess bell rang.

Todd and Noelle called a meeting of the Third-Grade Detectives at the swings.

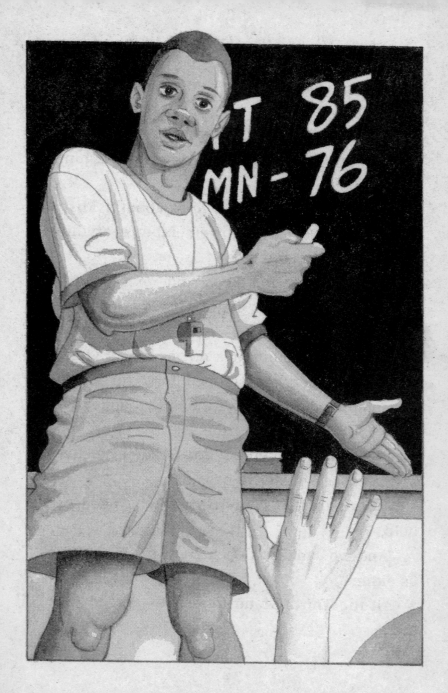

"We have to solve the secret code clue that Mr. Merlin gave us," Todd said. "If we don't, then Pops Verner will never get his pocket watch back."

"But Mr. Merlin isn't here to give us a hint!" Misty said.

"Then we'll just have to *think* about it, Misty," Todd said. "We'll have to remember everything that Mr. Merlin taught us."

"I miss Mr. Merlin," Leon said.

The rest of the Third-Grade Detectives nodded.

For a couple of minutes, no one said anything.

Then Amber Lee stepped forward. "As the former president of the former Dr. Smiley Fan Club, I say Todd's right," she said.

"We can't stop being Third-Grade Detectives just because Mr. Merlin has left.

"There are too many people who need our help.

"And we can't let Coach Hawkins brainwash us either!"

All the Third-Grade Detectives agreed with that.

They wanted to keep learning how police use science to solve crimes!

"Instead of working on the secret code clue in class, we'll work on it after school," Todd told them.

"Everyone can come to my house," Amber Lee said. "We'll go down to the basement."

"What about all those cobwebs?" Todd asked.

There was no way that he was going down to Amber Lee's basement!

"My parents just finished remodeling the basement," Amber Lee said. "There are no more cobwebs."

"Great!" Noelle said. "Will your mother have snacks for us?"

"I can't solve secret codes very well if I'm hungry," Leon said.

"I'll go to the office now and call her," Amber Lee said. "I'll ask her to make brownies and lemonade."

Now Todd felt better.

The Third-Grade Detectives were still together.

But Amber Lee's mother said they'd have to

wait until the next day to have their meeting.

She had other plans for that afternoon.

Todd couldn't believe it.

It was as if someone didn't want them to solve this mystery.

Todd decided that they couldn't waste a day.

He and Noelle would work on the secret code clue at his house after school.

In social studies, they talked about what kinds of sports are found in other countries.

In art, they drew pictures of people playing these sports.

Right before the final bell rang, Todd noticed something strange.

He got up from his desk and walked over to Mr. Merlin's bookshelf.

The *Big Black Code Book* was still there!

Why hadn't Mr. Merlin taken it with him when he left? Todd wondered.

All of a sudden, he knew the answer!

Mr. Merlin wanted to make sure that the Third-Grade Detectives could still solve their mysteries!

"Mr. Merlin lets us look for secret codes in this book," Todd said to Coach Hawkins. "I don't think he'd mind if I took it home with me tonight."

"Well, okay, but bring it back tomorrow," Coach Hawkins said.

The bell rang.

Coach Hawkins blew his whistle. "Line up at the door!" he shouted.

Todd grabbed the *Big Black Code Book* and got in line.

Suddenly he remembered what he had told Misty.

Mr. Merlin wanted them to solve secret codes to help them *think* better.

If he used the *Big Black Code Book*, would that be cheating? Todd wondered.

No! he quickly decided.

With the *Big Black Code Book*, the Third-Grade Detectives would be able to solve Pops Verner's mystery.

And that was the most important thing they had to do now!

Chapter Seven

"Is that Mr. Merlin's *Big Black Code Book*, Todd?" Noelle asked.

They were walking home from school.

"Yes! Coach Hawkins let me borrow it," Todd said. "I'm sure it's a clue!"

"A *clue*?" Noelle said.

Todd nodded. "Think about it, Noelle," he said.

"If Mr. Merlin is gone for good, then why was the *Big Black Code Book* still in the classroom?"

"Why?" Noelle asked.

"*Mr. Merlin left it there on purpose so we could use it to solve Pops Verner's mystery!*" Todd said.

"Oh yeah!" Noelle said.

When they got to Todd's house, they smelled brownies.

Sometimes Todd's grandmother baked him an after-school snack.

"They just came out of the oven," his grandmother said.

"Mmmm!" Noelle said.

"Thanks, Grandma," Todd said.

He and Noelle went to the kitchen.

"Your grandmother's brownies are always better than the ones that Amber Lee's mother makes," Noelle said.

"I agree," Todd said.

Todd poured two glasses of cold milk. He put two brownies each on a plate.

Together, they sat at the kitchen table.

Noelle looked at the *Big Black Code Book*. "It sure is *big*, isn't it?" she said. "It'll take us forever to go through it."

Todd sighed. "I know," he said.

"What if we're too late, Todd?" Noelle said. "What if the person who stole Pops Verner's pocket watch is no longer around by the time we solve the secret code clue?"

Todd wished Noelle would stop making it sound impossible.

For several minutes, they ate their brownies and drank their milk.

Then Todd said, "I just thought of something, Noelle. Maybe Mr. Merlin did give us a hint before he left."

Noelle looked puzzled. "I don't remember any hint," she said. She picked up a third brownie and started eating it.

"Mr. Merlin said that he and *Johnny* were going to give us a secret code clue,"

Todd explained. "And we asked him who Johnny was."

Noelle nodded. "Right. And Mr. Merlin said Johnny was one of his spy friends who made up secret codes," she said.

"Well, maybe Johnny's code is in this book," Todd said.

They started looking through Mr. Merlin's *Big Black Code Book*.

"There are some really interesting codes in here, Todd," Noelle said, "but nobody named Johnny made up one."

Finally they reached the last page in the book.

"Johannes Trithemius was the father of modern cryptography," Todd read. He looked up at Noelle. "I think that means he invented secret codes."

Noelle nodded. "I think so too," she said.

Todd looked back down at the page. "His most famous code is called the Square Table," he continued.

"It's made up of twenty-six alphabets.

"Each alphabet is slid one place to the left of the one above it."

Todd sighed.

He started to close the book.

Then he suddenly stopped. "Johannes Trithemius," he said. "*Johannes!* JOHNNY!"

Noelle blinked. "Do you think that's it?" she asked.

"I hope so," Todd said. "This code is our last chance."

He wrote out the Trithemius Square Table:

```
A B C D E F G H I J K L M N O P Q R S T U V W X Y Z
B C D E F G H I J K L M N O P Q R S T U V W X Y Z A
C D E F G H I J K L M N O P Q R S T U V W X Y Z A B
D E F G H I J K L M N O P Q R S T U V W X Y Z A B C
E F G H I J K L M N O P Q R S T U V W X Y Z A B C D
F G H I J K L M N O P Q R S T U V W X Y Z A B C D E
G H I J K L M N O P Q R S T U V W X Y Z A B C D E F
H I J K L M N O P Q R S T U V W X Y Z A B C D E F G
I J K L M N O P Q R S T U V W X Y Z A B C D E F G H
J K L M N O P Q R S T U V W X Y Z A B C D E F G H I
K L M N O P Q R S T U V W X Y Z A B C D E F G H I J
L M N O P Q R S T U V W X Y Z A B C D E F G H I J K
M N O P Q R S T U V W X Y Z A B C D E F G H I J K L
N O P Q R S T U V W X Y Z A B C D E F G H I J K L M
O P Q R S T U V W X Y Z A B C D E F G H I J K L M N
P Q R S T U V W X Y Z A B C D E F G H I J K L M N O
Q R S T U V W X Y Z A B C D E F G H I J K L M N O P
R S T U V W X Y Z A B C D E F G H I J K L M N O P Q
S T U V W X Y Z A B C D E F G H I J K L M N O P Q R
T U V W X Y Z A B C D E F G H I J K L M N O P Q R S
U V W X Y Z A B C D E F G H I J K L M N O P Q R S T
V W X Y Z A B C D E F G H I J K L M N O P Q R S T U
W X Y Z A B C D E F G H I J K L M N O P Q R S T U V
X Y Z A B C D E F G H I J K L M N O P Q R S T U V W
Y Z A B C D E F G H I J K L M N O P Q R S T U V W X
Z A B C D E F G H I J K L M N O P Q R S T U V W X Y
```

"The secret code clue that Mr. Merlin gave us is TIGUI BGZ I FYZPRB LYKFXMN," Todd said. "Let's see if it works."

Chapter Eight

T, the first letter of the secret code clue, was the same letter in the first alphabet, so Todd wrote down *T.*

"The first alphabet is called the clear alphabet," Todd explained. "You always use it to decode the secret message."

The next letter of the clue was *I,* so Todd found *I* in the second alphabet and looked above it in the first alphabet. He wrote down *H.*

"Let me try," Noelle said.

The third letter of the clue was *G.* Noelle found *G* in the third alphabet and looked above it in the first alphabet.

"*E,*" she said.

Todd wrote down *E.*

Together, they continued decoding the message.

When they finished, Todd said, *"There was a wooden witness!"*

"What does that mean?" Noelle asked.

Todd thought for a minute.

"The wooden statue, Noelle!" he said. "It was there when the crime was committed."

"Of course it was there, Todd," Noelle said. "Somebody hit Pops Verner over the head with it!"

But how could the wooden statue really be a witness? Todd wondered.

Witnesses talked.

They told police things they needed to know in order to solve a crime.

But a wooden statue couldn't talk.

It couldn't tell them anything about what had happened.

Todd sighed.

They had solved the secret code clue, but they hadn't solved Pops Verner's mystery.

"What are we going to do now?" Noelle asked.

"Mr. Merlin always gave us a second secret

code clue if we couldn't solve the mystery after the first clue.

"But Mr. Merlin is gone."

"We'll call him at his new school, Noelle," Todd said. "We'll tell him that we still need his help."

"What if he's not interested, Todd?" Noelle said. "What if he's too busy with his new pupils?"

Todd hadn't thought about that. Had Mr. Merlin already forgotten about the Third-Grade Detectives? he wondered.

"We'll do it anyway, Noelle. Maybe he doesn't like his new pupils as much as he liked us," Todd said. "We have to find a way to solve Pops Verner's mystery."

The next morning, Todd and Noelle got to school early.

They went to the principal's office.

Mrs. Franklin was sitting at her computer. "Good morning," she said. "Why the long faces?"

"We need to talk to Mr. Merlin at his new school," Todd said. "We want to ask him if he will give us another secret code clue."

"We hope he hasn't already forgotten us," Noelle added.

Mrs. Franklin wrinkled her brow.

"Mr. Merlin's not at a new school. He's just in the next town," she said.

"His mother was in a car accident. He drove over there to make sure she was all right.

"He didn't say anything about it to the class, because he didn't want to upset you."

Todd and Noelle looked at each other.

"We did it again," Todd said. "We made up stories in our heads."

Noelle nodded. "We got upset anyway, but for a different reason," she said.

"I have Mr. Merlin's cell phone number," Mrs. Franklin said.

"I'll call him now and let you talk to him for a few minutes."

"Great!" Todd said.

Mrs. Franklin dialed the number.

She asked Mr. Merlin about his mother and told him about some supplies he had ordered.

Then she said, "Two of the Third-Grade Detectives are here. They want to say something to you."

Mrs. Franklin handed Todd the telephone.

Todd told Mr. Merlin they all hoped his mother got well soon.

"Thank you, Todd. She's doing fine now, but I'll give her your get-well message," Mr. Merlin said, "and I'll be back at school tomorrow!"

Then Todd told Mr. Merlin that they had solved the first secret code clue. "But wooden statues can't talk, Mr. Merlin," he said. "We'll need another clue when you get back to help us solve Pops Verner's mystery."

"Well, Todd, the Trithemius Square Table is one of my favorite secret codes," Mr. Merlin said, "so I can give you a second clue now.

"It'll tell you how the statue can talk.

"Do you have a pencil and a piece of paper?"

Todd quickly got a pencil and a piece of paper from his backpack. "Ready," he said.

Mr. Merlin said, "LQSQ ID FVU JCJES."

Todd wrote it down.

"Since it may be hard to reach me for the next few hours, I'll even give you a hint," Mr. Merlin added. *Johnny is odd!"*

"May we work on it in class?" Todd asked.

"Yes. You may tell the substitute that I said it was okay for you to do that," Mr. Merlin said.

When Todd hung up the receiver, he said, "Let's surprise Mr. Merlin. Let's solve this mystery before he gets back tomorrow!"

Chapter Nine

Todd and Noelle hurried to their classroom.

"I have an announcement to make!" Todd said. "Mr. Merlin did not go to another school!

"His mother was in a car accident, but she's all right, and Mr. Merlin will be back tomorrow!" Everyone cheered.

Noelle turned to Coach Hawkins. "Mr. Merlin also said that it was fine with him if we tried to solve the second secret code clue before we started our other work," she told him.

"Okay," Coach Hawkins said.

"But we haven't solved the *first* secret code clue yet," Amber Lee said.

"Noelle and I solved it last night," Todd said. "We didn't have time to tell anyone."

"It's all my mother's fault," Amber Lee said.

"If we had met at my house yesterday, we could have solved it together!"

"We can still solve the *second* secret code clue together, Amber Lee," Todd said.

He told the class about Johannes Trithemius.

Then he walked to the chalkboard and wrote out the Trithemius Square Table:

A B C D E F G H I J K L M N O P Q R S T U V W X Y Z
B C D E F G H I J K L M N O P Q R S T U V W X Y Z A
C D E F G H I J K L M N O P Q R S T U V W X Y Z A B
D E F G H I J K L M N O P Q R S T U V W X Y Z A B C
E F G H I J K L M N O P Q R S T U V W X Y Z A B C D
F G H I J K L M N O P Q R S T U V W X Y Z A B C D E
G H I J K L M N O P Q R S T U V W X Y Z A B C D E F
H I J K L M N O P Q R S T U V W X Y Z A B C D E F G
I J K L M N O P Q R S T U V W X Y Z A B C D E F G H
J K L M N O P Q R S T U V W X Y Z A B C D E F G H I
K L M N O P Q R S T U V W X Y Z A B C D E F G H I J
L M N O P Q R S T U V W X Y Z A B C D E F G H I J K
M N O P Q R S T U V W X Y Z A B C D E F G H I J K L
N O P Q R S T U V W X Y Z A B C D E F G H I J K L M
O P Q R S T U V W X Y Z A B C D E F G H I J K L M N
P Q R S T U V W X Y Z A B C D E F G H I J K L M N O
Q R S T U V W X Y Z A B C D E F G H I J K L M N O P

```
R S T U V W X Y Z A B C D E F G H I J K L M N O P Q
S T U V W X Y Z A B C D E F G H I J K L M N O P Q R
T U V W X Y Z A B C D E F G H I J K L M N O P Q R S
U V W X Y Z A B C D E F G H I J K L M N O P Q R S T
V W X Y Z A B C D E F G H I J K L M N O P Q R S T U
W X Y Z A B C D E F G H I J K L M N O P Q R S T U V
X Y Z A B C D E F G H I J K L M N O P Q R S T U V W
Y Z A B C D E F G H I J K L M N O P Q R S T U V W X
Z A B C D E F G H I J K L M N O P Q R S T U V W X Y
```

"The first secret code clue was: TIGUI BGZ I FYZPRB LYKFXMN," Todd said.

He showed the class how he and Noelle had decoded it.

Noelle explained what the clue meant. "The wooden statue was there when the crime was committed," she said. *"It was the wooden witness!"*

"Statues can't talk," Leon said. "That won't help us solve the mystery."

The rest of the class agreed.

"That's why Mr. Merlin gave us a second secret code clue," Todd said.

Todd wrote it on the chalkboard: LQSQ ID FVU JCJES.

"Did he also give you a hint?" Misty asked.

"Yes," Noelle said. "He said that Johnny was odd!"

"Mr. Merlin's hints are too hard," Amber Lee said. "I'm going to give up and do something else."

Several of the Third-Grade Detectives agreed with her.

Todd couldn't believe this was happening.

Usually Amber Lee wanted to be the first one to solve the mystery.

"Mr. Merlin wants us to *think* about it, Amber Lee," Todd said. "He'll be disappointed in us if we don't."

"I don't care, Todd," Amber Lee said.

"I take back everything I said.

"I was only interested in being a Third-Grade Detective so I could be like Dr. Smiley.

"But she isn't here to be a role model, so I don't want to be a Third-Grade Detective anymore."

"I don't think I want to be one either," Misty said.

So that's it, Todd realized. They're still upset that Dr. Smiley left.

He knew he had to do something fast before the Third-Grade Detectives disappeared right in front of him.

"What if Dr. Smiley offers you a job when you grow up, Amber Lee?" Todd asked. "How can you work for her if you stop doing detective work?"

Amber Lee thought about that for a minute. "You're right. If she offered anybody a job, it would be me," she said. "I still need to keep in practice."

Todd relaxed. At least for the time being, he decided, they were still the Third-Grade Detectives.

"I think the first thing we have to figure out is what the word 'odd' means," Todd said.

Coach Hawkins took a book off a shelf. "This is a thesaurus," he said. "It gives you a list of words that mean the same thing."

He turned to the Os and found the word "odd." "It means funny, strange, weird," he said. "It also means unequal or uneven. Like *odd* numbers and *even* numbers on sports jerseys."

Todd thought for a minute. Odd numbers.

Even numbers. He looked at the Trithemius Square Table on the chalkboard.

"That's it!" he shouted. "I know how to solve the second secret code clue!"

Chapter Ten

Todd pointed to the secret code clue: LQSQ ID FVU JCJES.

"*L* would be *L*," he said, "because the first letter of the clue is always the same letter in the first alphabet.

"But Mr. Merlin's hint said that Johnny was odd, so that means you're supposed to use the *odd*-numbered alphabets."

"Oh, I get it!" Noelle said. *"You use every other alphabet!"*

"Exactly!" Todd said.

"The second letter in the clue is *Q*.

"So you go down to the third alphabet and find *Q*.

"Then you look above it in the first alphabet and you find *O*.

"The first two letters of the message are *LO*."

Using only the *odd*-numbered alphabets, Todd decoded the rest of the clue: LOOK AT THE RINGS.

"That's not fair!" Leon said. He was looking at his hands. "If you don't wear rings, how can you look at them?"

"Mr. Merlin isn't talking about rings you wear on your fingers," Todd said. "I think he's talking about *tree* rings!"

"But which tree?" Noelle said.

"I don't know," Todd said sadly.

The next day, all of the Third-Grade Detectives were in their classroom bright and early.

Everyone had made signs to welcome Mr. Merlin back to school.

Amber Lee and Misty put them up around the room.

"Thank you all very much," Mr. Merlin said. "I missed you, too!"

"We solved the secret code clue, Mr. Merlin," Todd said, "but we don't know which tree rings to look at."

"Yeah! There are broken trees all over town!" Misty said. "And they all have rings!"

"I know. We're going to study a cross section of one of the trees that blew down in the woods behind the school," Mr. Merlin said.

"This morning I sawed off a tree stump so we'd have a nice smooth circle to look at.

"After we've finished, I'll tell you which 'tree' I was talking about."

Mr. Merlin and the Third-Grade Detectives left their classroom and walked to the woods.

The class gathered around the tree stump.

"Tree rings give us a record of the local climate and history during the life of the tree," Mr. Merlin began.

"We can study the rings to learn if the tree lived through floods, drought, insect attacks, or forest fires.

"Some trees are hundreds of years old.

"Some trees are thousands of years old.

"Tree rings give us information that is often not available from other sources.

"If the rings are thick, the tree grew in a place that gets a lot of rain.

"If the rings are thin, the tree grew in a place that doesn't get much rain.

"If the rings are neither thick nor thin, that means the tree grew in a place where the amount of rain during a year is somewhere between a little and a lot."

"These rings are thick," Todd said. "That's because it rains a lot where we live."

"That's right, Todd," Mr. Merlin said.

"The light ring is called early wood. It grows fast during the spring and the early summer.

"The dark ring is called late wood. It grows more slowly.

"The two rings together represent one year of growth.

"Let's count them to find out the age of this tree."

The Third-Grade Detectives started counting the rings.

When they got to the center, they had counted to 246.

"That means this tree started from a seed soon after 1758," Mr. Merlin said.

"The United States wasn't even a country then," Amber Lee said.

"That's right," Mr. Merlin said. He sighed. "It's really a shame this tree can't keep growing."

They looked at the stump and found the rings that showed how big the tree was when important events happened in the United States:

1776. America declared its independence from Great Britain.

1865. The American Civil War ended.

1927. Charles Lindbergh flew across the Atlantic.

1945. The Second World War ended.

1963. President John F. Kennedy was assassinated in Dallas.

2001. The World Trade Center towers in New York City were destroyed by terrorists.

"It's interesting to read a tree!" Leon said. "I like reading trees better than books."

Mr. Merlin smiled. "I promised you I'd tell you which tree I was talking about in the second secret code clue," he said. "It's—"

"Wait, Mr. Merlin!" Todd said. "Let us guess."

"Okay," Mr. Merlin said.

"Pops Verner was hit over the head with a little wooden statue," Todd told the class.

"That statue was once part of a tree.

"I think if we look at its rings, we can solve the mystery."

From behind his back, Mr. Merlin produced the wooden statue.

It was in two pieces.

"What happened to it?" Noelle cried.

"The police let me saw it in half," Mr. Merlin said.

He looked at Todd. "You're right," he said. "I told them that if the Third-Grade Detectives could read the statue's rings, they could solve Pops Verner's mystery."

Todd grinned.

Mr. Merlin and the Third-Grade Detectives went back to their classroom.

They divided into two groups.

Mr. Merlin gave the top part of the statue to Todd's group.

He gave the bottom part of the statue to Amber Lee's group.

"Let's find out what year it started from a seed," Noelle whispered.

"That won't help us solve the mystery," Todd said.

"Anyway, that would be hard to do, since the outer layers have been whittled away."

"Well, what do we need to look for?" Misty asked.

"The size of the rings," Todd replied. "Thick, thin, or somewhere in between."

Todd's group studied the rings for several minutes.

Finally Todd said, "They're not thick, and they're not thin."

"They're somewhere in between," Noelle said.

"Right," Todd said. "Pops Verner has three suspects. Joe, Phil, and Bobby. We need to find out where they're from."

Todd asked Mr. Merlin if he could make an important telephone call.

Mr. Merlin said he could.

Todd hurried to the principal's office and called Pops Verner.

When he got back to the classroom, he gathered his group together.

"Joe's from Utah, Phil's from Arkansas, and Bobby's from Florida," he said. "I looked up all three states in the almanac."

"Utah is dry and Florida is wet, but Arkansas is moderate.

"Arkansas gets more rain than Utah, but not as much as Florida.

"The rings on trees in Arkansas would probably be somewhere between thick and thin!

"So I think this wood came from Arkansas.

"And I think it was Phil who whittled this wooden statue and hit Pops Verner over the head so he could rob the store. He must have seen the pocket watch and taken it."

"Mr. Merlin! Mr. Merlin!" Amber Lee cried. "We've solved the mystery."

Todd couldn't believe it.

He should have worked faster.

"What's your solution, Amber Lee?" Mr. Merlin said.

"1954!" Amber Lee said.

"Well, that may be when the tree started from a seed," Mr. Merlin said, "but . . ."

Todd waved his hand.

"We have an answer too, Mr. Merlin," he said.

Todd told Mr. Merlin about Phil and why he thought the wood came from Arkansas.

"I think that's the right answer," Mr. Merlin said. "We'll give the information to the police, and they can go to Greene's Department Store and talk to Phil."

Two days later Pops Verner came to their class.

"I want to thank the Third-Grade Detectives for helping me get my pocket watch back," he said.

"When the police told Phil they thought he whittled the statue from a piece of wood he brought from Arkansas, he confessed to hiding in the store so he could rob it.

"He had already sold what he had stolen, but he still had my pocket watch in his pocket!"

"Why did he leave the statue at the scene of the crime?" Noelle asked. "It was evidence."

"Crooks aren't always very bright, Noelle," Pops Verner said. "He probably didn't think that something he had whittled would solve a crime."

"We're glad you got your pocket watch back," Noelle said.

"Thanks," Pops Verner said. "But you got something back too."

Just then Dr. Smiley walked into the classroom.

The Third-Grade Detectives were so surprised they didn't know what to say.

"I'm not leaving after all," Dr. Smiley announced. "I decided the new job wasn't worth being away from the Third-Grade Detectives."

Everyone in the class cheered.

Todd looked at Noelle. "After school let's look for a mystery that Dr. Smiley will have to help us solve," he said.

"That's a good idea," Noelle said. "We need to keep her so busy that she won't ever think about leaving again!"

Talking Trees

Check the library or Internet Web sites to learn as much as possible about dendrochronology— the science of tree rings. (There are many related Web sites on the Internet.) Then find a tree that has just been cut down. You can often do this where people have cleared land to build new houses. Have someone (your parents or your teacher) cut a "thick slice" from the trunk.

In *The Secret of the Wooden Witness*, Mr. Merlin told the Third-Grade Detectives how tree rings provide a record of local climate during the life of a tree. Count your tree rings. Remember to count a light ring and a dark ring as one year. In what year did your tree begin life? What was happening in your town that year? Find the ring that was formed during the year when you were born. Think of some other important things that have happened in your life (or in your parents' lives). Find the tree rings that were formed during that time. Write a weather history of your area by "reading" the rings. When was there a lot of rain? (Hint: thicker rings) When was there a drought? (Hint: thinner rings) Was there ever a forest fire? (Hint: Look for fire-scar wounds—sometimes known as "catface.")

THIRD-GRADE DETECTIVES

Everyone in the third grade loves the new teacher, Mr. Merlin.
Mr. Merlin used to be a spy, and he knows all about secret codes and the strange and gross ways the police solve mysteries.

YOU CAN HELP DECODE THE CLUES AND SOLVE THE MYSTERY IN THESE OTHER STORIES ABOUT THE THIRD-GRADE DETECTIVES:

Coming Soon: #9 The Case of the Sweaty Bank Robber

ADDIN PAPERBACKS • Simon & Schuster Children's Publishing • www.SimonSaysKids.com

Ready-for-Chapters